Gary Glory
the amazing
Flying Fish

Bright Sparks ☆

"I'm bored!" said Gary Glory swimming in and out of the seaweed.

He went to find Buster Blowfish, but Buster was practising making himself **BIG**,
then **BIGGER** and then **SMALL**, then SMALLER.

He went to find Pearl the Curl, but she was busy crimping her fins.

"Nobody wants to play with me," said Gary crossly.

"Can't you entertain yourself for five minutes?" asked Pearl.

"Actually," said Gary, a light suddenly coming into his eye, "I can entertain myself."
Pearl looked at him nervously. "Now Gary, you should leave those birds alone."

"Phooey, why should I?" asked Gary rudely, and he shot off.

"Oh dear," sighed Pearl.

She stopped her crimping and swam away to find Buster.

Horace and Warble were sitting in their favourite tree on their favourite branch
which hung far out over the sea. This was where they always sat,
snoozing and gossiping in the sunshine, passing the time of day.

"Look!" said Warble suddenly, sitting up straight.

"I don't see anything," mumbled Horace, and he sank back into his doze. "There it is again!" cried
Warble and this time they both heard a blood-curdling yell: **"YEEEEEEAAAAAARGH!"**

Then they saw it - a mysterious, silvery creature, flashing in the sunlight.

It leaped out of the ocean with a great leer on its face, turned a perfect somersault in the air...

...and disappeared again beneath the waves.

"**SQUAWK!**" cried Horace and Warble in fright. They both fell backwards off their perch and plummeted **DOWN DOWN** DOWN through the air and landed in the sea with a great **KERPLOSH!**

Oscar Octopus was taking some of the little ones for a nature ramble through the coral.

Suddenly he saw two extraordinary creatures hurtling towards them.

"Take cover!" cried Oscar, putting out all of his arms to shield the little fish.

Gary Glory hid behind a rock and laughed until he cried.

"Their faces!" he puffed, slapping his sides. "Those dozy birds - I get them every time!"

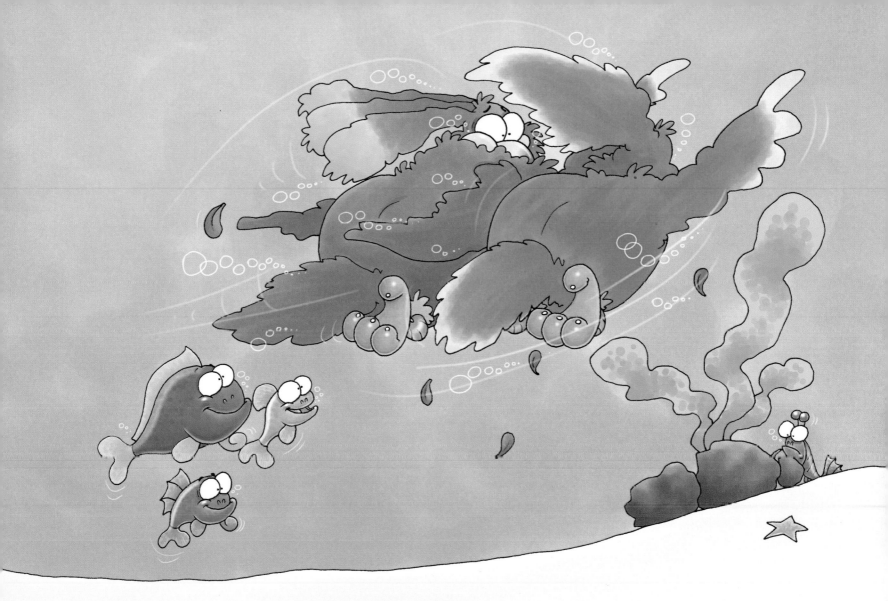

"They're going to get you one day," said Pearl sternly, swimming up from behind.
"I don't think so," said Gary scornfully. "They're far too stupid to get me!"

When they had recovered, Horace and Warble talked late into the night.

"It was a bird," said Horace. "No, no," insisted Warble. "It was an amazing flying fish."

"Fish can't *jump* that high!" "This one can," said Warble.

"It *must* have special breathing powers out of the water."

"Or else," said Horace, "it's a bird with special breathing powers under the water!"

The birds thought long and hard. "Either way," said Warble at last, "it's a very special creature and we shouldn't keep it to ourselves."

"You mean ..." breathed Horace. "That's right," said Warble importantly. "We should announce our spectacular discovery to the newspapers. But first, we have to catch it."

Gary was so pleased with yesterday's success, that the next day he teased the birds again. He looked up through the waves and there were Horace and Warble, sitting on their usual branch, getting a suntan.

Gary took a deep breath and prepared to make the leap. He did a splendid somersault high in the sky - **"YEEEEEEAAAAAARGH!"** - and then blinked in surprise. For instead of landing back in the water, he had landed in a great big net!

"Got him!" cried Warble.

"You're going to make us famous!" said Horace.

"Famous AND rich," said Warble.

They tied Gary into their nest, and then flew off to tell the newspapers about their amazing discovery: the astonishing **FLYING-SWIMMING FISH-BIRD!** Left behind all alone, Gary was really scared. He knew he couldn't survive long out of water.

Luckily for Gary, Oscar Octopus had seen what had happened.
He rushed off to find Buster and Pearl. "What can we do?" cried Pearl.
"We must rescue him, but he's up a tree and fish can't climb trees!"
"No," said Buster. "But crabs can."

They hurried to find Scuttle the Crab. Scuttle was in a bad temper, as always.
"Nobody ever comes to call unless they want something," he grumbled.
But all the same, he agreed to help.

Slowly and carefully Scuttle began to make his way up the tree trunk.
The branch where the nest rested was not very high. In no time he had reached the nest
and was untying poor Gary, who by this time was turning blue in the face.

"Throw him down!" cried Buster from below. "There's no time to lose!"

Scuttle took Gary gently between his claws and threw him as far as he could. But a sudden gust of wind blew him inland. Instead of landing in the sea below, Gary landed in a rockpool on the beach. "Help!" he gasped. "Where am I?"

Suddenly Scuttle appeared, peering over the edge of the pool. "Sorry about that," he said.
"I was never a very good shot. You'll just have to wait for a wave to carry you back to sea.
The tide's coming in so you shouldn't have to wait long."

Gary sat impatiently in the pool waiting for the right wave. It was like being in prison, with rock walls in every direction. Suddenly a small wave broke into the pool. "The tide's coming in!" yelled Scuttle. "Wait for a really big wave and then *jump* with it!" Wave after wave rolled into the pool. The water crashed around the rocks and poor Gary was thrown all over the place.

He held on for a particularly big wave and then he *LEAPED* up into it.
The water rushed past him like a tornado, pulling and pushing him at the same time - and
when he opened his eyes he was safely back in the sea.

"Stand back," said Oscar. "He's coming round."

"Oh Gary, you scared us!" cried Pearl, and she gave him a big kiss.

"Wow!" cried Buster. "That looked like great fun!"

"Well, young man, what have you learned from all this?" asked Oscar sternly.

Gary looked around the familiar faces and gave a big sigh of relief.

"No more teasing the birds," he promised.

Horace and Warble returned to the shore with
helicopters and television cameras, reporters and photographers.
Everyone wanted to see the astonishing **FLYING-SWIMMING FISH-BIRD!**

But all they found was an empty nest.

This is a Bright Sparks Book
First published in 2000

Bright Sparks
Queen Street House
4 Queen Street
Bath BA1 1HE, UK

This book was created by
small world creations ltd
Tetbury,UK

Written by Janet Allison Brown
Illustrated by Matt Ward
Designed by Sarah Lever

© Parragon 2000

Printed in Spain

ISBN 1 - 84250 - 028 - 7